The Stable Where Jesus Was Born

The Stable Where Jesus Was Born

by RHONDA GOWLER GREENE

illustrated by SUSAN GABER

✳

SCHOLASTIC INC.

New York Toronto London Auckland Sydney
Mexico City New Delhi Hong Kong

ISBN 0-439-47019-6

Text copyright © 1999 by Rhonda Gowler Greene.
Illustrations copyright © 1999 by Susan Gaber. All rights reserved.
Published by Scholastic Inc., 555 Broadway, New York, NY 10012,
by arrangement with Atheneum Books for Young Readers, an imprint of
Simon & Schuster Children's Publishing Division.
SCHOLASTIC and associated logos are trademarks
and/or registered trademarks of Scholastic Inc.

12 11 10 9 8 7 6 5 4 3 2 1   2 3 4 5/0

Printed in the U.S.A.   14

First Scholastic printing, December 2000

Book design by Michael Nelson
The text of this book is set in Guardi Roman.
The illustrations are rendered in acrylic on Bristol board.

For Matt
⁓R. G. G.

To Joanne
⁓S. G.

This is the father, Joseph, so tall,
who cared for the baby and animals all,
but mostly the mother, Mary by name.

These are the shepherds who came in the night,
who left flocks of sheep in their hurry and flight
and wished well the father, Joseph, so tall.

This is the angel who said, "Fear not!"
who spoke of a birth in a glorious spot
and sent fast the shepherds who came in the night.

This is the town called Bethlehem
where families gathered and filled every inn,
beheld by the angel who said, "Fear not!"

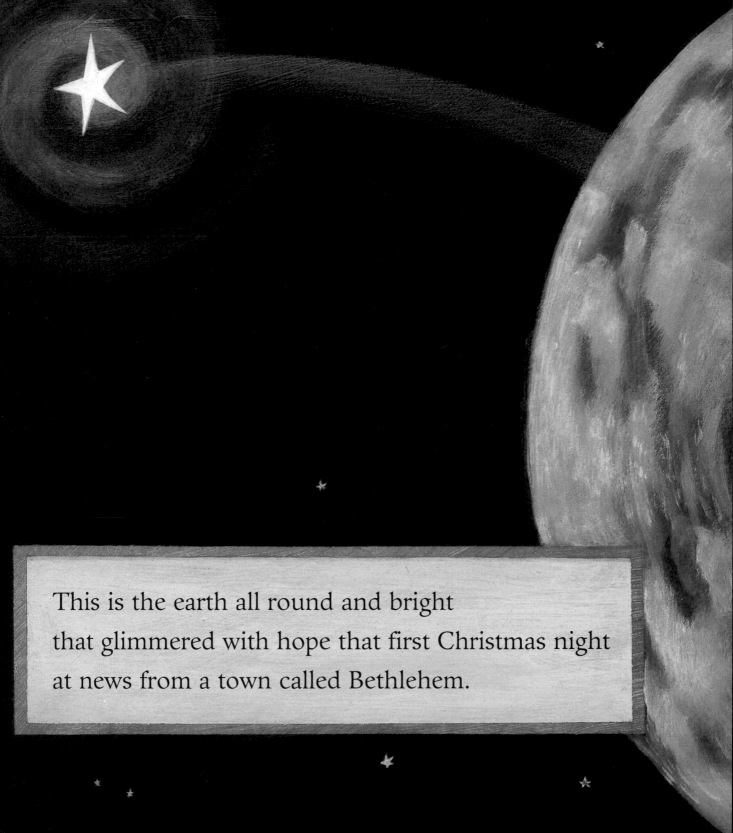

This is the earth all round and bright
that glimmered with hope that first Christmas night
at news from a town called Bethlehem.

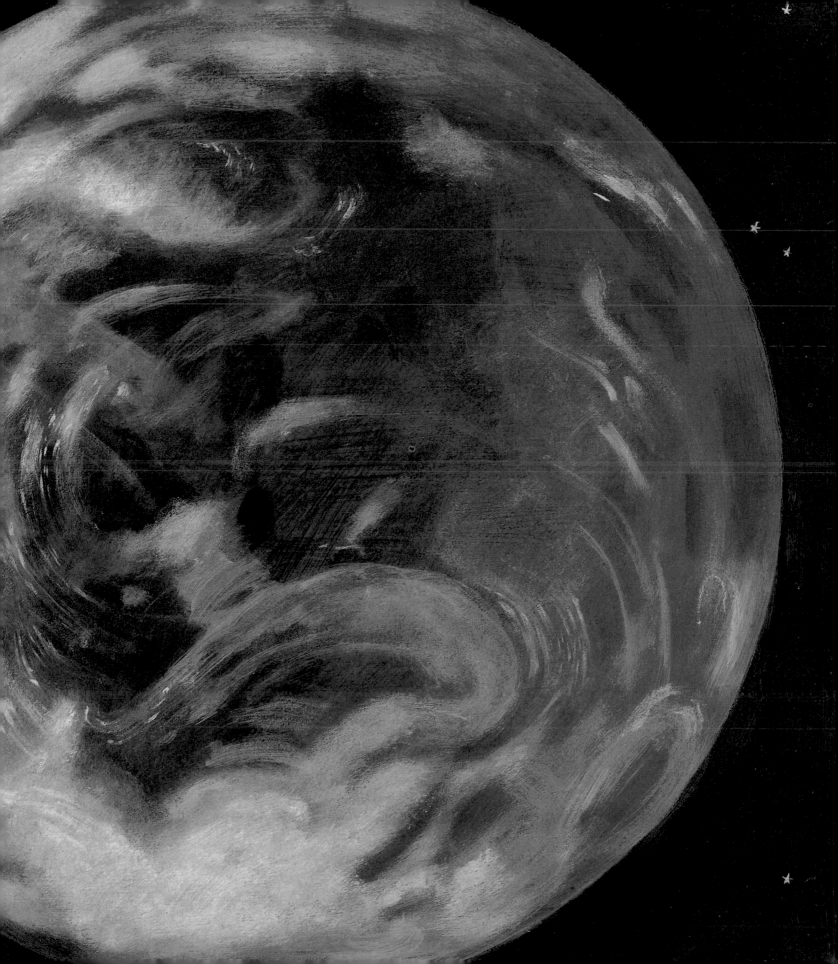

This is the baby in swaddling clothes,
the small precious baby, the one whom God chose
to come to the earth all round and bright
that glimmered with hope that first Christmas night

at news from a town called Bethlehem
where families gathered and filled every inn,

beheld by the angel who said, "Fear not!"
who spoke of a birth in a glorious spot

and sent fast the shepherds who came in the night,
who left flocks of sheep in their hurry and flight

and wished well the father, Joseph, so tall,
who cared for the baby and animals all,

but mostly the mother, Mary by name,
the mother of Jesus she became,

❧

who sat near the cow in the sweet-smelling hay,
the cat and her kittens and three mice at play,

❧